Venetia
Lake Michigan's Treasure

Written by Gay Lyn Birkholz

Illustrated by Linda K. Williamson

Strategic Book Publishing

Strategic Book Publishing
An imprint of Strategic Book Group
P.O. Box 333
Durham CT 06422
www.StrategicBookGroup.com

ISBN 978-1-60860-129-5

Illustrated by Linda K. Williamson

Printed in the United States of America

Dedication

Thank you to our wonderful mother, Sue, for inspiring a passion for reading; to our father, Hank, for instilling the awe, respect, and love for Lake Michigan; and to Aunt Marilyn for teaching me the beauty of seeing treasure in rubbish.

Venetia felt so proud sitting on the shelf and hearing all the wonderful comments coming from the shoppers about her.

"Oh, Mom, look at the pretty bottle. I've never seen anything like it. Let's try it."

You see, Venetia was a new beautiful red glass bottle that the cola company had recently introduced to the market.

Venetia felt good that her design and beautiful color were helping her company attract new customers and sell more of its delicious cola. She was delighted she contained a tasty, refreshing beverage for her customers in a unique and pleasing vessel.

One day, a family purchased Venetia. They were on their way to Lake Michigan and needed drinks to complete their picnic. Venetia was so excited at the thought of bringing joy to the family. She truly felt fulfilled in her life.

Venetia and the family were having a super day on the lake. The sun was shining and warm, Lake Michigan was smooth with gently rolling waves. Venetia was so happy in the cooler being chilled by the ice. The waves rocking Venetia were causing the cola to slosh and bubble. It tickled! Everyone was having fun, laughing, soaking up the sunshine, partaking of good food, swimming, and being together.

Even though the family had been eating and drinking all afternoon, Venetia had not yet been plucked from the cooler. The little girl, Isabella, who had been swimming most of the day, finally came out of the water, her skin dimpled and prune-like. Venetia overheard the girl tell her mother she had been saving "the red bottle" for a special moment, and now, after all the swimming, she was so thirsty and ready for her treat. Isabella picked Venetia out of the cooler to have with her lunch. Because she had allowed herself to get so parched, she couldn't wait to dry off to take a big drink of Venetia's cool, smooth cola to quench her thirst.

After Isabella had taken a sip and started to put the bottle down, it slipped from her wet, dimpled hands and cracked down on the rail of the boat, shattering Venetia into many pieces and bouncing the fragments into Lake Michigan.

The experience sent Venetia into shock.

"It wasn't supposed to happen this way! My life was planned—I was to be returned to the store, recycled, and refilled so I could bring a pleasurable beverage to someone else."

Venetia felt so confused and betrayed.

When Venetia tried to assess the damage, she found pieces of herself scattering every which way in the

water. One larger piece of her was left, and sadly, the rest of the small shards were swirling away.

Venetia immediately planned how she could gather the pieces of herself. However, she soon realized she would never have her old life again.

As she swirled in the water, she cried out to God, "How could you let this happen? I know the little girl did not intend to break me, but my life has been taken from me. What good am I to anyone now?"

From far, far away, Venetia seemed to hear a voice. She could only assume it was God answering.

"Venetia, remember, I am with you always. I will take this tragedy and turn it into something good."

The words were comforting, but Venetia kept asking herself how broken pieces of glass could possibly be put to good use.

Venetia heard the roar of the boat motors. The sounds were moving away, so she realized the boats were returning to the docks. The sun began setting, it was getting dark, and the water temperature was dropping. Venetia had never felt so alone, cold, scared, or helpless in all her life. She could do nothing but let the one piece of her that was left float in the water. It was so scary as fish and seaweed brushed by her. Venetia finally learned she had to relax and simply go with the experience, as to fight it would tangle her more securely in the seaweed. When she relaxed, she would pass through the seaweed or gently brush by the fish. If she relaxed, nothing else was fighting her.

When Venetia finally floated to the bottom of the lake's floor, the sand was comforting and soft. She lost any sense of time. At the bottom of the big lake, Venetia couldn't tell day from night. She only knew that she had been there a long time. Venetia wondered why she had not heard any boats for several days until she remembered a conversation the adults had on the boat when they were celebrating the Labor Day holiday, the end of summer. That

meant the kids were back in school, and everyone was busy with other activities. No one had time to come to the lake, and summer was virtually over.

So, Venetia resigned herself to living at the bottom of the lake for an eternity. She never believed this was why she had been created, but she was stuck. What else could she do? Venetia tried to make the best of her situation. She came to appreciate the beauty that surrounded her at the bottom of Lake Michigan. There were hundreds of species of fish, all different types and colors of plants and interesting rock formations. However, still it was difficult for Venetia to be stuck. She was not serving any purpose or offering any service. But, try as she might, she could not make herself move! She was embedded in the sand and at these depths even her beauty could not be appreciated as it was too dark to see her vibrant red hues.

All of a sudden, the floor of Lake Michigan rumbled. Venetia had never felt this sensation before. The rumblings increased in strength and volume! The sand was shifting, and it was if the lake was completely flopping over, turning itself inside out. One huge wave of the water arose and picked up Venetia.

"I'm free, I'm free, and I'm not stuck anymore!"

Venetia was so happy with her newfound freedom.

But, tossing in the massive waves was a ride like none that Venetia had ever been on. It was truly the ride of her life. She was thrown, tossed, and tumbled. She had no idea where she was until she felt herself being thrown against rocks. "Ouch!"

It hurt so much to be pitched in the sand and against other rocks, but as it was happening, Venetia could feel her outer layer changing, being chipped away. Venetia again cried out to God. "I thought being broken was bad, and then I thought being stuck at the bottom of Lake Michigan was worse, but Lord, this is unbearable! Please help me. What have I done to deserve this?"

Linda K Williamson

Even over the roar of the water and rocks hitting together, Venetia heard God.

"Venetia, remember I told you that I am with you always. I will turn this into something good."

Venetia was so hurt. She knew what God said had to be true, but how could this possibly be for her good? How could being broken apart and scraped up be to her benefit?

And so the winter storms had begun, and the wind blew and blew tossing Venetia over and over again. When a lull in the wind came, it gave Venetia a chance to look herself over. To her astonishment, she saw that her surface appeared completely different

Lord K williamson

than she had ever looked before. There were dents and dimples all over her from hitting other rocks.

Venetia whispered to herself, "I thought I looked bad when I was broken into a hundred pieces, but now I'm broken and mangled. I don't even recognize myself. There is nothing of *me* left."

And so the winter continued. Venetia never would have thought she could have made it through, but she did, day after day through the pounding and grinding. It still hurt, but she had become somewhat numb to the discomfort. When she allowed herself to think about it, she could still hear those words, "I will be with you always, and I will turn this for your good."

The winds slowed down, and Venetia could even feel the water temperature was rising. The sun felt warmer and closer, and the waves rolled more gently. Venetia sensed she had been gradually moving into more shallow water. One day, a wave pushed her onto the beach. *Ah, warm sand*, she sighed. The stillness of being out of the water was strange.

"What can I do now?" she asked herself.

Many days passed this way with Venetia on the beach. Spring had come, the sun had been shining for several days straight, and things were both calm and peaceful. On an especially nice day, people started visiting the beach. It wasn't warm enough to

sunbathe yet, but it was fun to see everyone flying kites and enjoying the beach. The warm weather had been nice long enough to bring the "glassers" out.

Venetia could feel from the vibrations of the sand granules that a woman and little girl were coming her way.

She heard the young girl, Jenna, ask her mother, "What are you putting in the bucket?"

Her mother answered that she was gathering pieces of glass that had washed on shore. Jenna offered to help but wanted to know why they were doing this. The mother explained to her daughter that with the beautiful pieces of beach glass they collected, they

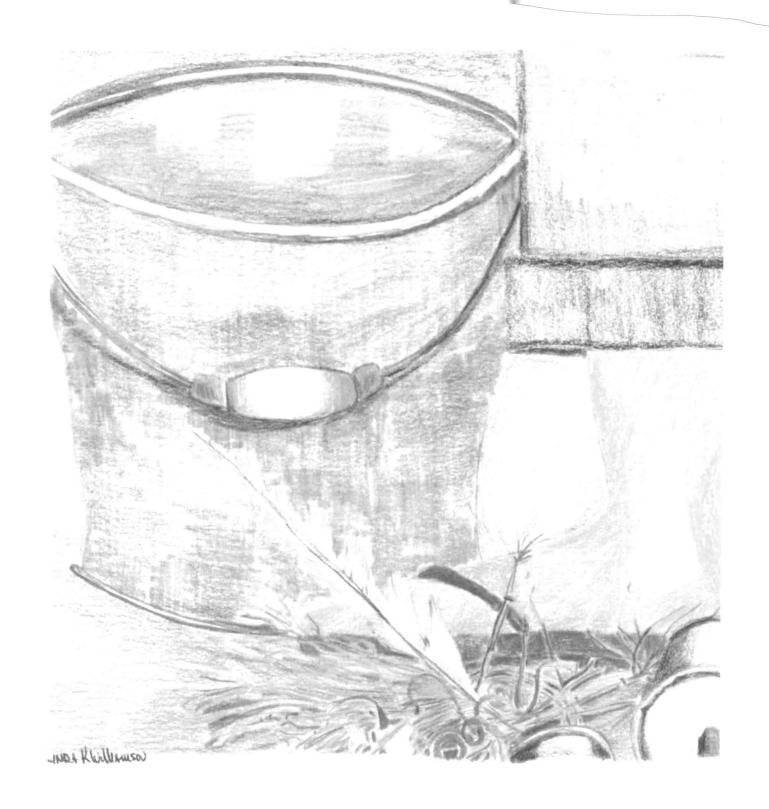

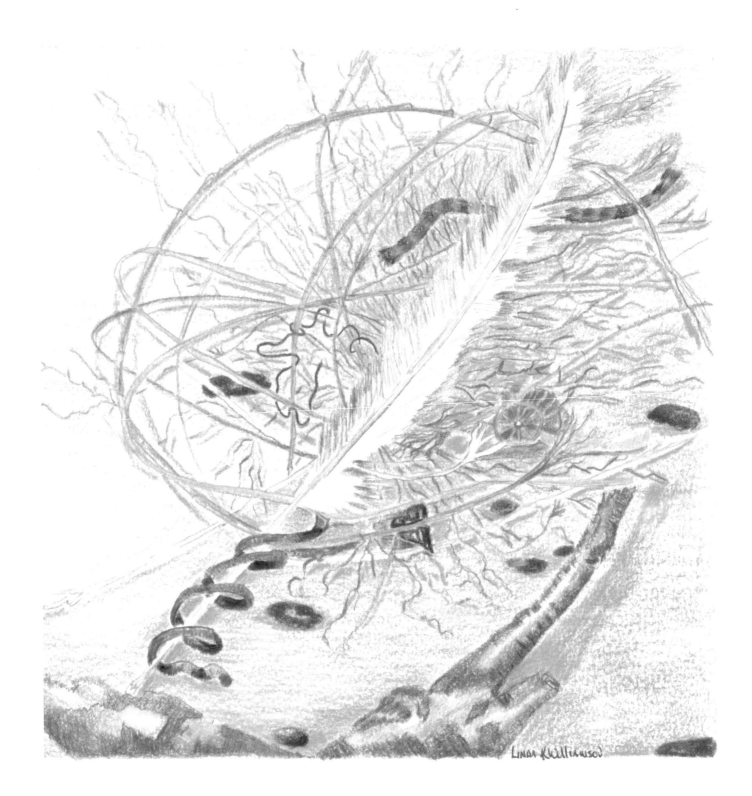

could make crafts or just collect the pieces and put them in a jar to remember their fun times on vacation.

"Mommy, they look like jewels!" exclaimed Jenna.

"I know," replied her mother, "They do, and in a way, they are."

"What do you mean?" asked Jenna.

Her mother went on to explain, "Well, ordinary pieces of glass get dumped or thrown somewhere in the big lake. Through the process of them being ground against the sand and other rocks, they are 'polished' by nature, just as a jeweler polishes fine gems. We are looking for polished pieces of glass."

As they walked along, they came upon Venetia and Jenna spotted her.

"Mom, look! A red piece of glass! We'll have to take this. I've found a red piece of beach glass! Isn't she beautiful?"

Venetia was overjoyed to hear those words. It felt so good to bring joy to someone again, and finally, she was going to be put to good use!

"It is beautiful, and red glass is so rare to find, but we can't keep it," replied Jenna's mother. "Why not? It's so beautiful!" cried Jenna.

"Well, it is beautiful, but look, it is not fully polished yet. It just has dents and scrapes but not a

smoothly polished surface. We'll throw it back so the polishing process can be completed," explained the mother.

And with that, the mother threw Venetia far out into Lake Michigan again.

Venetia was heartsick.

"Lord, how could you let her do that to me? Haven't I been faithful? Haven't I suffered enough? Haven't I done all I could do? Why was I placed upon the beach if not to be rescued?"

And so the days went on. Venetia knew the routine by now, the grinding, the pain, the darkness of being underwater, and the confusion of rolling constantly with

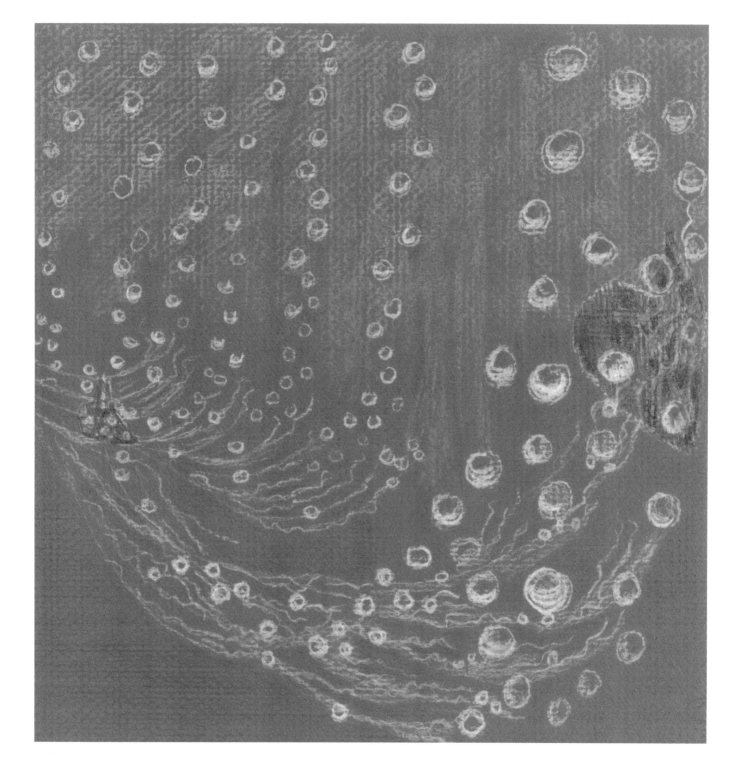

the waves not knowing where they would transport her.

The spring storms arrived, and the change in the winds churned up the lake and carried Venetia far out away from the shore. Venetia was devastated. Her thoughts were on how close she had been to being rescued and if she would be able to hang on and survive this again. Still, there was that voice in her head that assured her, "I am with you always, I am still with you, and I will turn this for your good. You were not quite finished yet." Venetia knew it had to be God, and even though she was furious with him for letting this happen, how could she believe anything else?

So, Venetia endured the seasons far out in the

middle of Lake Michigan. Finally, she felt the waves churn and change direction. She knew it was the familiar trip back to the shore.

This trip was longer and in many ways harder this year. Last year it seemed to Venetia to be a straight shot to the shore, but this year she seemed to go forty yards forward and twenty yards back. Venetia was so frustrated that the only thing she could do was to give in and let the water take her where it chose. She could never let go of those feelings of betrayal. She knew what God had spoken to her, but how, how could she ever be of any use? There were simply no answers. None of it made any sense.

This year, as the journey to the shoreline was more complicated, Venetia did not make it until summertime. As soon as she washed up on the beach, she felt the warm sand and the blistering sun. The light and warmth did feel good, and to hear all the people laughing and having fun was soothing, but Venetia still felt so dejected that she couldn't enjoy it as fully as the first time. A frightening thought kept recurring to her: *What if someone does find me, and they just throw me back in again?*

In her frantic state of mind, Venetia had not bothered to look herself over. If she did, she would have discovered she was magnificently polished from

Linda K Williamson

point to point. Even her edges were rounded and smooth. Her color had gone from a bright scarlet to a beautiful muted red with an opaque-like finish.

"Wow!" Venetia exclaimed after working up the courage to really examine herself. "I don't look anything like I used to. And I don't *feel* anything like I used to. It's hard to admit, but all of that polishing has made me more beautiful than I ever thought possible."

Venetia got over her surprise and looked around her surroundings. She again felt stabs of disappointment. Yes, she had been brought back up on the beach, but she was buried under seaweed and further examination of her environment revealed that trash

was also caught in the sea grass. How could anyone ever find her under all of this mess?

As the days passed, Venetia could feel the beachcombers and glassers walk right past her. She could hear the other beach glass that had been picked up clanging in the buckets as the glassers happened by. Disappointment and resentment consumed her. As the summer wore on, Venetia was convinced that this now was her destiny, to get so close to being rescued only for the fall storms to come again and take her back out to the lake. She wouldn't even allow herself to dream of "what if" anymore.

Then, on one of the last days of summer when the

waves had been calm for several days and the beach grass surrounding Venetia had dried out completely and deteriorated, the little girl, Jenna, and her mother were glassing for the last time of the season.

They were walking along enjoying the time together and offering their goodbyes to the beach for the year when the mother remarked, "Jenna, you have really become a good glasser. Your eyes are sharp and you find more pieces of beach glass than I do now."

Just as she said that, a hint of something caught Jenna's eye. The sun's rays had hit Venetia just right as she was entangled in the pile of dried up beach grass and trash. Those piles of dried beach grass

always reminded Jenna of sagebrush piles they saw out west, only these were smaller. Normally, Jenna wouldn't dare touch these slimy heaps as they were dirty and there was even a fish carcass in this one, but she saw something red, she knew she did.

Jenna found a piece of driftwood and shoved the beach grass to the side. There, almost waiting to be found, was the most beautiful piece of polished-to-perfection red glass!

"Mom, look, isn't she beautiful? I bet it's the same piece of red glass we found last year and threw back in the lake."

Jenna's mother replied, "I don't know. It's pretty

unlikely that the lake would bring the same piece of glass back to the same beach, but as lucky as you have been to find two pieces of red glass in your short life when I haven't found any, maybe it is possible. She is a beauty. What are you going to do with her, Jenna? Maybe you could put her into that mosaic table we are working on."

But Jenna knew the moment she found the red glass she wasn't going to squander her on furniture.

"No, Mom, she is so beautiful, so rare. She looks just like those Venetian glass beads we saw in the bead store the other day. Why don't we make her the centerpiece of the necklace you are making?"

Jenna's mother replied, "Jenna, that is a wonderful idea! I haven't been able to finish that necklace because I couldn't find the perfect bead, but she is it!"

Venetia could hardly believe what she was hearing. Imagine, her, a common glass bottle becoming the focal point in a gem necklace, bringing so much joy over and over each time it was worn.

At last, Venetia understood those words, "I will work this for your good." This could only be a miracle from God. What made it even more miraculous was the knowledge that Venetia now knew the other scattered pieces of herself would bring pleasure to so many artists, crafters, and admirers of their works when these gifted individuals found the pieces of Venetia and put them to use in their artistic creations.

Sometimes, one's purpose or the power of God is not readily evident. As Venetia discovered, all it takes is faith and patience and everything turns out brilliantly in the end!

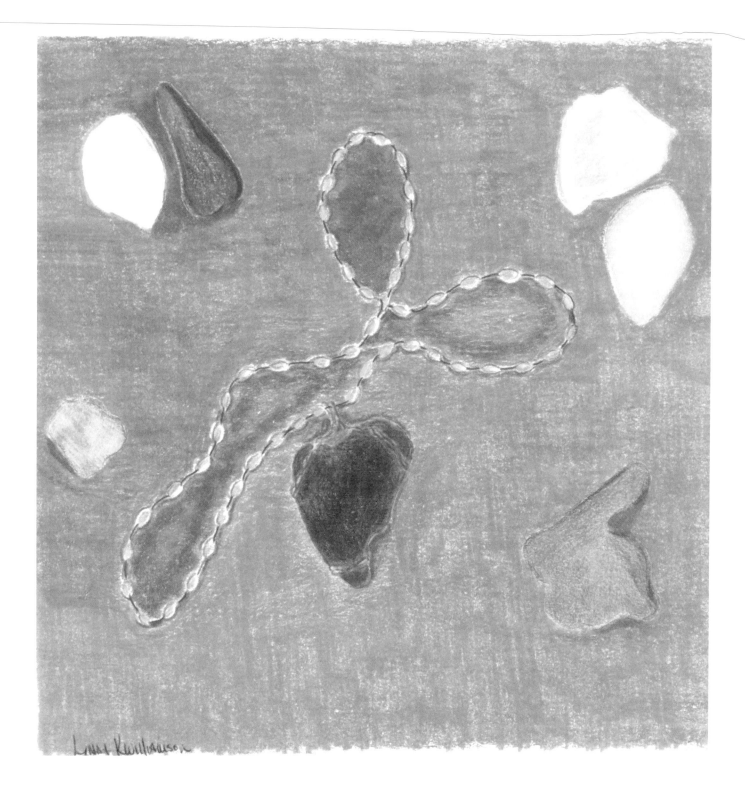

CPSIA information can be obtained
at www.ICGtesting.com
Printed in the USA
LVIW022324070413
328039LV00001B

* 9 7 8 1 6 0 8 6 0 1 2 9 5 *